Captain Blownaparte
Pirate Superstar!

by Helga Hopkins
Illustrated by David Benham

First published as an eBook in 2013
Paperback edition published in 2018

contact@blownaparte.com

ISBN-13: 978-1720738008
ISBN-10: 1720738009

Captain Blownaparte™
Pirate Superstar!

by Helga Hopkins & David Benham

This is the story of the legendary Pirate, Captain Blownaparte, who got his name after a big battle against his arch enemy...

A cannonball nearly hit Captain Blownaparte. It was a very close shave and half his clothes were blown away!

The rest of him was left smouldering and his hair standing up on end! Sproggie, the cabin boy shouted: 'Help! The Captain has been blown apart!' So that's how the Captain got his funny name.

One day, a big storm came along and a very wet parrot was blown onto the ship.

Luckily little Sproggie looked after him, and after a few days Captain Blownaparte asked the parrot if he wanted to fly back to the jungle. 'Oh no! I'm staying with you', squawked the parrot. 'Every famous pirate needs a lucky parrot on his shoulder!' Captain Blownaparte was tickled pink with his new friend, and decided to name him 'Prosper'.

Prosper was a very clever parrot, and each week he read the Gold Treasure Magazine, so he knew where all the treasure ships were sailing on the ocean. Prosper was always busy reading, and Captain Blownaparte was counting gold coins – this was his favourite hobby.

On deck, the ship's crew were playing football as usual. But they all hoped that the Captain wouldn't want to join in.

'That cutlass he uses for a wooden leg will be the death of us,' grumbled one patched up pirate. 'Every time he joins the team, he slices up all our footballs!'

'Not to mention all of us!' said another poor pirate who had a rather grubby band-aid on his nose!

Sproggie longed to play football too, but unfortunately, he had to help polish all the silverware with Pirate Tidy, the ship's cleanest and most fussy crew member.

Suddenly, Prosper squawked loudly in the Captain's ear after reading that Purplebeard was taking a load of poor captured parrots back to England to sell as caged pets. 'Oh No! Not more parrots,' moaned the Captain.

But Prosper quickly trilled that Purplebeard's ship was also carrying a huge chest of extra large gold coins! 'Oh well, in that case we'll have to save the gold coins, er… I mean the parrots!' said Captain Blownaparte, looking very jolly all of a sudden.

Dropping anchor in a small harbour, Sproggie was sent to find out when Purplebeard was setting sail.

Sproggie sneaked into a dark old tavern and hid under Purplebeard's table so he could listen to his plans. But unfortunately Purplebeard saw the little boy and pulled him out by his ear. 'Just looking for coins!' cried a frightened Sproggie.

'I'll give you coins!' roared Purplebeard, and threw him out of the tavern window. Luckily Sproggie had heard all he wanted to know, so he jumped up, wiped his nose and quickly set off back to the ship.

Later, Captain Blownaparte caught up with Purplebeard's ship.

ut the nasty pirate shouted across the waves: 'You can't shoot your canons at my ship – if you sink me, all the parrots will drown!'

'Those bloomin' parrots!' muttered Captain Blownaparte, and stamped his foot down hard.

But as usual, he'd forgotten that his leg was a cutlass, and now it was stuck firmly in the deck!

'All hands to help the Captain – he's got stuck again!' yelled Sproggie. So the crew dropped everything to pull the Captain's leg free.

Then suddenly, Prosper had a brilliant idea. 'We'll fill the sliced up footballs with sticky toffee and fire them at Purplebeard's ship instead of the cannon balls! – The toffee will stick everything together and we can save the parrots!' 'And get the gold!' shrieked Captain Blownaparte.

'What a great idea,' said one of the crew. 'I ate some of the ship's toffee this morning and it was so sticky it pulled all my teeth out!'

So Captain Blownaparte ordered the crew to fill the footballs with sticky toffee, and they rained them down on Purplebeard's ship...

...covering him and his men in a horrible sticky mess!

Every move Purplebeard made got worse and worse.
It was a very sticky situation.

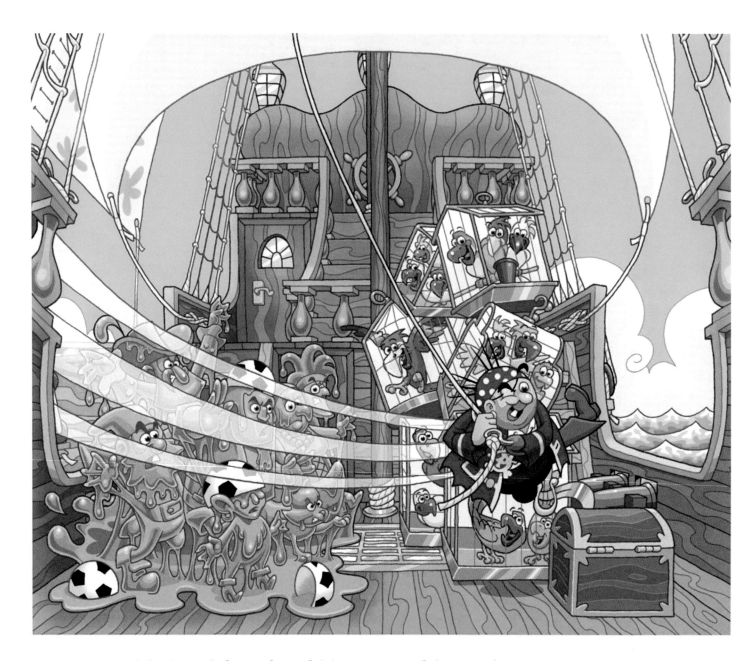

With Purplebeard and his crew safely stuck together, Captain Blownaparte swung aboard to save the parrots and collect the gold.

Purplebeard looked on helplessly with toffee all over him and daggers in his eyes. 'Try and chew your way out of this,' said Captain Blownaparte as he dug his arms into a huge chest of sparkling coins.

Back on board their ship, the crew celebrated with a game of football while Captain Blownaparte counted the gold.

Meanwhile, Sproggie and Prosper quickly opened the cages of the saved parrots, who swooped off back to the jungle with a squawk of thanks to Captain Blownaparte.

'Don't you want to go with your friends?' the Captain asked
Prosper. 'Not on your life,' said the parrot. 'I'm coming on your
next adventure!' 'Bloomin' parrots!' giggled Captain Blownaparte.

And as the sun set, Captain Blownaparte was the happiest Captain on the seven seas.

PEDRO

ROSIE

CAPTAIN
BLOWNAPARTE

PROSPER

SPROGGIE

SPIKE

PIRATE TIDY

TURNIP

ALFREDO

SWISS SEPP

Made in the USA
Las Vegas, NV
18 August 2021